# The Adventures of Avery Ann-Space

Leah MacKenzie

Balboa Press books may be ordered through booksellers or by contacting:

Balboa Press
A Division of Hay House
1663 Liberty Drive
Bloomington, IN 47403
www.balboapress.com
1 (877) 407-4847

ISBN: 978-1-5043-3528-7 (sc)
ISBN: 978-1-5043-3529-4 (e)
Library of Congress Control Number: 2015910256

Print information available on the last page.

Balboa Press rev. date: 11/03/2015

BALBOA.
PRESS
A DIVISION OF HAY HOUSE

# Dedication Page

Lovingly dedicated to Joy Haack, Dave Dunahay, Mr. Gettling, Sally Cassidy, Paul Monaco, Gene Brodeur, Cindy Bell, Skye Wolf MacGregor, and Donnalee Baudry.

You all have a special place in my heart. I will be forever grateful for your protection, encouragement, guidance and support. You believed in me and helped me when I needed it most. Thank you for making me feel safe, special and loved.

# Author Expression of Appreciation

How many people does it take to create a book? A team of many! Major "thank you" and much gratitude to the following people for supporting the creation of *The Adventures of Avery Ann: Space:*

Bob & Maureen Atchison, Tom Gail, Cody Atchison, Perrine Solara & Justin Smelser, Leslie Grasa, Becky Bauer & Dave Griffith, Cynthia Slon, Angel Pittman, John Ellis, Martha McDonald, Jay Abramovitz, Marianne Monson, Ron & Apollo Johnson, Shannon Vincent, and Tara Riley Snyder. Bateman Larkin Certified Public Accountants, P.C.

Kid's illustrations: Jennifer, Vance & Vivian Atchison, Kristin P. & Caden Cash, Meghan Rudisill & Lila Broadrup, Kelly, Sean, Cate & Ellie Neill, Jennifer, Gabriel & Violet Rike, John & Henry Barrios, Sarah & Avery Houston, Julie Kearns & Meridel Kearns-Stanley, Aimee Ten Eyck-Schaffer & Isabelle Schaffer, and Erin & Ava Gail.

Review committee: Clare Trapp, Susie Ten Eyck-Johnson, Donnalee Baudry, and Anne Gail. Thanks for helping me fine-tune the adventure.

Liz Overstreet: Thanks for being a fantastic layout consultant and story reviewer. Having you involved spared me stress.

Lari Silva: I don't publish my work without first passing it by you. Thank you for sharing your editing skills enabling the flow of *The Adventures of Avery Ann*.

Olivia Cole: Your illustrations are stunning. I truly enjoyed our collaboration in bringing Avery Ann's space adventure to life. Here's to more adventures!

Love & blessings,
Leah

Avery Ann's teacher asks the class, "Who wants to share for tomorrow's show-and-tell?"

Avery Ann grins when she is chosen. "I'll bring my rock collection," she says proudly.

Bouncing on her pogo stick in her driveway, Avery Ann tells Blue, "I would love some space rocks for my rock collection." She can't help dreaming of space travel.

"Great idea, Blondie. Let's go find some," says Butterfly Blue, her beloved sidekick.

Jumping higher and higher into the air, Avery Ann lifts off into the sky. She zooms through the clouds, flies past a plane, zips past a satellite, and comes to a skidding stop on the moon with Butterfly Blue at her side.

Shaking on the landing, she proclaims, "That's one small step for tomboys, one giant leap for kids." Exploring the moonscape, Avery Ann sees four sets of multi-colored bug eyes staring at her. One of the aliens waddles up and touches her with its gooey, three-fingered hand. "You're it," he says, then turns and catches up with his friends who are running to hide.

Hide-and-go-seek," whispers a delighted Butterfly Blue.
Tip-toeing around craters, she playfully tags each new friend, ending the game in giggles.

"I'm searching for space rocks for my rock collection," she tells them when the game is over.

One of them gives her a rock that matches the color of its bug eyes. "This rainbow rock will add color to your collection."

Her new friend then points to a distant crater. "You should meet the Crystal Man. He knows all about rocks."

"Thanks, I will," says Avery Ann. Waving goodbye to her new playmates, she heads out to find the Crystal Man.

A squeaky voice whispers from a mountain peak. Avery Ann follows the voice up a lunar cliff. At the top, she spots a rock that looks like a crab. Frozen in shock, she watches it crawl away.

"Blondie, that would make a great rock for your collection," calls out Butterfly Blue.

As Avery Ann chases the crab rock, it turns and asks her, "Can I help you?"
"I'm looking for space rocks for show-and-tell. I've never seen a rock that walks and talks. Want to come to school with me?" she asks.
"Yes I do!" the crab rock replies.
"Great! I am excited for you to meet my friends," says Avery Ann.

Just then, a storm hits the solar system. Swirling wind picks Avery Ann up and carries her to the far side of the moon.

She touches down on a sheet of ice where one-legged creatures are playing hockey. The action stops as the space creatures circle around to meet her.

"We are short one player. Want to play with us?" asks the captain of the Yacron hockey team.

Skating on the ice, she traps the puck, spins and hits a slap shot, scoring a goal right before the buzzer screams: game over!

"Avery Ann, you helped us win! This "Most Valuable Player" rock is for you," says the coach.

"Cool! I will add this MVP rock to my collection."

"Congrats, Blondie! We need to get going if you want to make it home for show-and-tell," warns Butterfly Blue.

"Where can we find the Crystal Man?" she asks the team.

"That way, in the massive old lava flow," they point out.

"Go, Yacrons!" Avery Ann shouts as she glides away.

Nearing the lava tube, Avery Ann sees a giant, glowing man walking towards her. Shielding her eyes from his brightness, she can feel his warmth.

"I've been looking for you, Crystal Man."

"Nice to meet you, Avery Ann. How can I help?"

"I would like one more space rock for my rock collection," Avery Ann explains.

"You know, crystals have special powers," he says. "How about a crystal instead of another rock for your collection?"

"Yes! I'd love a crystal," says Avery Ann eagerly.

The Crystal Man breaks two crystals from his body and hands them to her. "This large crystal is for your rock collection and will shine when needed. This tiny crystal is for your charm bracelet."

Avery Ann kisses him on his cheek and gushes, "Thank you, Crystal Man!"

Crystal Man can't hide his blush.

On her pogo stick ready to leap home, Avery Ann is suddenly pulled into a black hole!

Lost in darkness, Butterfly Blue says, "Trust the crystals, Blondie!"
Holding her large crystal, Avery Ann asks it, "Will you help us?"
The large crystal glows brightly, lighting up the hole. Avery Ann feels something touch her head.
"Grab the rope," calls a voice from above.

Holding onto the rope, she is lifted out of the black hole and placed safely back on the moon by a team of astronauts. "We were fixing the space station when we saw your light," says an astronaut.

Avery Ann high-fives the space explorers. "Thank you for rescuing me! It's so cool being in space with astronauts!"

"You're welcome, Avery Ann," they say, waving goodbye. The astronauts float back to the space station while Avery Ann searches for her pogo stick.

Just then, a meteorite crashes to the ground next to her. It is followed by another, and another. She dodges, ducks and hides from the wild rocks.

Butterfly Blue warns, "We need to go now! Forget about the pogo stick, Avery Ann."

"Oh, okay," she says sadly.

Needing a different way home, Avery Ann jumps onto a comet passing by, leaps onto an asteroid heading for earth, and rides it home. She lands with a thud on the ground. "Wow! What an awesome ride," squeals Avery Ann. Mission accomplished, she adds the otherworldly rocks to her collection.

The next morning, her pogo stick mysteriously appears in her yard. "Sweet!" she says, and then happily rides to school.

Avery Ann's rock collection is the star of show-and-tell. The classroom glows bright from the crystal and the kids play Duck-Duck-Goose with the crab rock.
"I love your rock collection," says Butterfly Blue.
"It's out of this world!" agrees Avery Ann.

# Avery Ann's Fun Facts Notebook

Moon drawn by: Violet Rike    Age: 6

**Moon:** The Moon is made up of rock. The Moon is hot during the day and cold at night, like a desert here on Earth. The Moon has lots of holes on it. The holes on the Moon are called craters and made when comets and asteroids crash into it. When I was walking on the Moon, I climbed in and around large and small craters. The aliens I played Hide and Seek with told me the earth's ocean tides are caused by the gravitational pull of the moon.

Alien drawn by: Vance Atchison    Age: 8

**Aliens:** Some people don't believe in aliens, but I know they are real because they are my friends. We played a very exciting game of Hide and Seek on the moon. Aliens are people who live in space and fly UFOs (Unidentified Flying Objects). Next time I go to the Moon, my alien friends promised to take me on a ride in their UFO! I am so excited about flying in a UFO!

Lila Broadrup

Crystals drawn by: Lila Broadrup    Age: 5

**Crystals:** The Crystal Man showed me all kinds of crystals. Crystals come in all shapes, sizes and colors. I especially liked the crystals with several colors. The Crystal Man told me crystals are made when liquids inside the Earth cool and become hard. The Crystal Man also told me crystals have healing powers. I think it's so cool that I have crystals from the Moon in my rock collection.

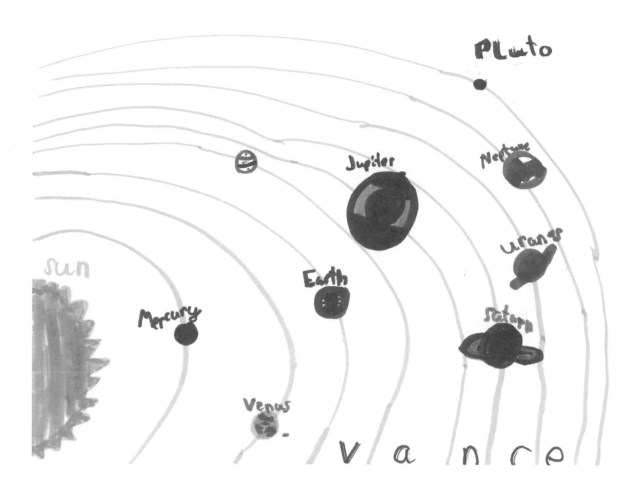

Solar System drawn by: Vance Atchison    Age: 8

**Solar System:** Traveling on my pogo stick through space, I zipped through the solar system. The solar system is big and includes the Sun, planets, comets, asteroids, meteoroids and moons. The nine planets in the solar system are Mercury, Venus, Earth, Mars, Jupiter, Saturn, Uranus, Neptune and Pluto. I giggle every time I hear the name Uranus. On my next trip to space, I'm going to visit a planet.

Lava tube drawn by: Henry Barrios    Age: 6

**Lava Tube:** Lava tubes on the Moon are ditches that used to carry lava from volcanoes. Lava tubes were made when the outside hardened and the lava inside them still flowed.

Black Hole drawn by: Vivian Atchison    Age: 4

**Black Hole:** A black hole is super strong and pulls anything that comes close to it into it. Black Holes are so dark you can't see anything. I was a little scared when I was sucked into the black hole. I was so glad the astronauts saved me!

Space Station drawn by: Avery Houston    Age: 5

**International Space Station:** The International Space Station is where astronauts from around the world live and work while in space. It is a science lab where the astronauts collect information about space. The International Space Station is the biggest object ever flown into space. The International Space Station is so big it can be seen from Earth at night.

Astronaut drawn by: Isabelle Schaffer    Age: 5

**Astronauts:** An astronaut is a person who works in space. Astronauts are men and women scientists. The Astronauts who pulled me out of the Black Hole, told me they wear diapers under their space suits, which made me laugh. Neil Armstrong is a famous astronaut because he was the first person to walk on the Moon.

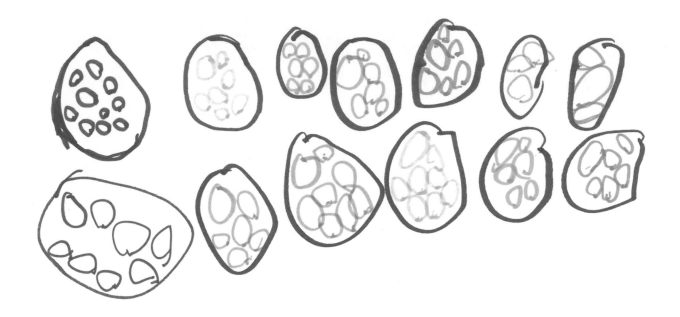

Meteoroid drawn by: Ellie Neill    Age: 5

**Meteoroid:** A meteoroid is a small rock in the solar system. A shooting star is a meteoroid entering the Earth's atmosphere. I make a wish every time I see a shooting star.

Meteorite drawn by: Cate Neill    Age: 8

**Meteorite:** A meteor that crashes into the Earth's ground.

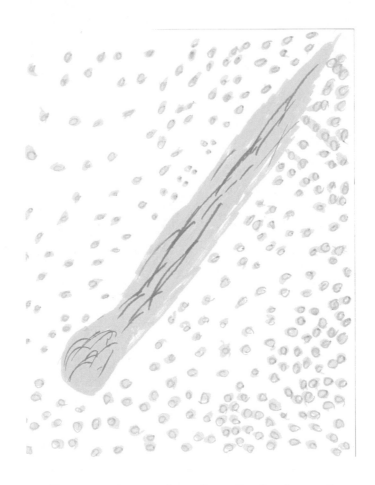

Comet drawn by: Ava Gail   Age: 8

**Comet:** When I jumped onto a comet to get off the moon, I felt ice, dust and small rocky particles...ouch! Comets move around the Sun and have a fuzzy outline and tail.

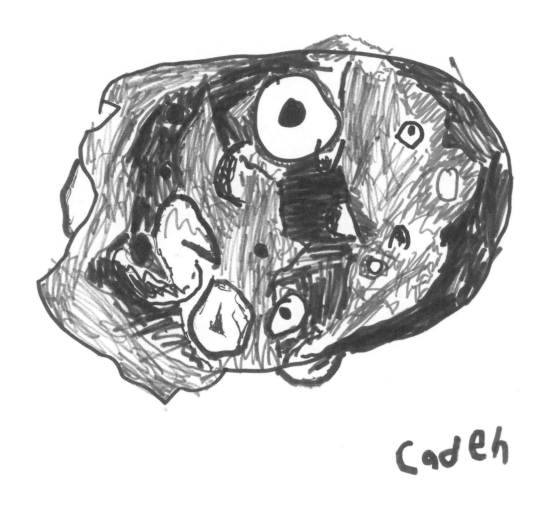

Cadeh

Asteroid drawn by: Caden Cash    Age: 6

**Asteroid**: When I rode the asteroid, I could feel it was made of rock and metal. Some asteroids are made of other stuff too. Asteroids fly around the Sun and are really big.

Satellite drawn by: Meridel Kearns-Stanley    Age 6

**Satellite:** There are man-made Satellites, which ride on rockets to get into space. These satellites collect information about space for scientists and look like bright stars from Earth. There are also natural satellites, like the Moon. Natural satellites are from space.

Printed in the United States
By Bookmasters